Just One Night

J.M. GOODRICH

Just One Night

Copyright © 2022 J.M. Goodrich

Cover by Haelah Rice Covers

J.M. Goodrich is a native of Michigan's beautiful upper peninsula. She loves spending time outdoors as much as she can with her family when she's not reading or writing. She has been published in several different anthologies and novels of her own. She has written stories of romance, fantasy, and horror. In addition to her love of writing, she has a passion for music, and an obsession with The Beatles.

Nina

I FELT LIKE SUCH A FAILURE. And let's face it, I am. No matter what my mom tells me. What else would you call someone who is not only failing most of their classes at college, but just got dumped by their long term boyfriend? Not that I believed in fairy tales or anything, but I was sure Tom and I were going to go the distance, whatever that meant.I thought that we would have a long, happy life together.

But he had other plans. It seemed as if he was on a mission to get in the pants of every girl on campus. Everyone seemed to know it but me. I was so humiliated when I found out. I couldn't show my face around campus anymore so I ran home to my mother's house.

She welcomed me home with open arms and a look of pity in her eyes.

It only made me feel worse.

I hated feeling like I was letting her down. My mom did everything she possibly could for me. She never had the opportunity to attend college herself, and so she worked extra hard to save up to make sure that I was able to go. She was so proud of me when I got accepted. It was like both our dreams were coming true.

But now I blew it by pretty much failing every class that I took. I tried, I really did. I was just . . . distracted a little.

By life.

And boys.

Stupid, I know. Really stupid. But now I was more determined than ever to work hard and finally be someone my mother could be proud of.

But right now I had to drive downtown to the bakery. Once a week my mom and I would make dinner together and order dessert from George down at the bakery. No one baked better than that man. And everyone knew it.

He not only had his bakery constantly filled with cakes and cookies, donuts and pastries, but he also made the most beautiful wedding cakes I had ever seen.

He also catered any party, school function or graduation, or anything else anyone planned, and he never blinked an eye. He was happy to do it and absolutely loved his job.

I don't know when the man had time to sleep.

But right now I was thankful for him. While my mom and I were pretty decent cooks, we couldn't bake to save our lives.

It wasn't pretty.

So while mom was washing the dishes we used to cook dinner, I grabbed my purse and keys and headed out the door.

Nina

⌇

I DROVE to the bakery across town to pick up our dessert. As much as we loved those sweet treats, neither my mom or I could bake. Like, at all. Everything we attempted either turned into a gooey or a burnt mess. Never anything even slightly edible. Luckily there was a bakery in town that was absolutely amazing. The baked goods were top notch and the owners were the friendliest people I've ever met.

"Good afternoon, Nina," George greeted me warmly as I entered the shop. George and his wife Amy had owned the bakery together for as long as I could remember.

"Hi George." I returned his smile.

"Your pie is just about done. We're putting the finishing touches on it right now."

I took a seat at one of the many small tables and started thinking of a plan for getting my life together. Whatever it was, it had to be good and it had to be fast. I was getting too old to be living life like this.

I was so deep in my own thoughts that I hadn't noticed the second customer that had entered the shop at first. As the man stepped up to the counter to give his order, I felt that there was something familiar about him. But I couldn't place where I would know him from. Until he turned to look my way.

When I saw his face, I froze.

Brandon Cole. The man who had spent making all four years of high school an absolute living hell for me. It was almost like he went out of his way to make my life miserable back then.

And here he was, standing in front of me.

I hated him.

I had heard that he moved away after high school. I remember the feeling of relief that washed over me at hearing that news. Finally, I'd be able to live my life without worrying myself sick thinking about what he would do next. Not that college had been an amazing experience for me or anything, but it was a hell of a lot better than dealing with Brandon Cole daily.

"Nina Haywood? Is that really you?"

Shit, he had spotted me. He was staring directly at

me now. Not wanting to speak to him, I quickly looked down and played with my phone, pretending to text someone. Maybe he'll just get the hint and go away if I ignore him.

"Nina?" Now he was right at my table.

Why couldn't he take the hint that I didn't want anything to do with him?

Slowly, I raised my eyes to meet his. "Brandon," I said, trying to keep any and all emotion out of my voice.

"So it is you," he laughed as he took a seat at my table. "How have you been? It's been a long time."

Not long enough, I thought. I wanted to disappear. I quickly glanced at the bakery counter hoping George was done with my order so I could grab it and have an excuse to get out of here. But he was nowhere to be seen, Neither was my pie. I groaned.

Brandon cleared his throat and I looked up at him. I could tell from his expression that he was still waiting for me to answer him. "I've been doing alright," I lied. He didn't need to know the truth. Hopefully I'd never have to see his face again after leaving the bakery.

Although this is a small town. . .

Hoping he would be satisfied with that answer and move on, I turned my attention back to my phone. But Brandon stayed seated at my table.

"Not much of a talker, huh?" he laughed.

Anger was beginning to build inside me. I did not want to deal with this today, or any day. "Why would I?" I asked, a little harshly.

A confused look spread across his face. "Did I . . . have I done something to you?" His voice sounded so innocent. How could he not know? High school wasn't that far away.

I scoffed. "Seriously? You don't remember?" I sat back in my chair, folding my arms across my chest.

Brandon seemed to be searching his memory. "I can't remember anything that I . . ."

I cut him off. "You used to bully me. Throughout high school."

"I used to bully you?"

"Yes."

He scratched his head. "I honestly don't remember that. I'm sorry. I'm sorry if I did that though. I don't know why I would have done that . . ."

"I don't either, but every single day you and your little group of friends would make my life a living hell. And from what I could tell, you all enjoyed it." I said, standing up. Tears began to prick at the back of my eyes. The last thing I wanted was for him to see me cry.

Brandon opened his mouth to reply but before he could get a single word out, George called my name to let me know my order was ready. I didn't waste a single second walking over to the counter, ignoring Brandon.

"I added some homemade pistachio ice cream," he winked. "Thought you could use it."

George, you dear sweet man. "I sure could." I brightened up a bit. "Thank you so much George. I know Mom will really appreciate it."

"Give her my best," he called as I headed out the front door with my goodies.

I had gotten about two steps from my car door when I felt a hand on my arm. Turning, I found that Brandon had followed me. "What do you want?" I asked. I had been so close to escaping.

"I want to apologize," he answered, taking a step back and shoving his hands in his front pockets. "I didn't mean to hurt you back then. I was a stupid kid. I thought that we were just all having fun," he shrugged his shoulders.

"That's no excuse." And I was definitely not having fun then.

"I know," he lowered his eyes to the ground. "I don't know what I was thinking. But why does it still bother you? It's been years. I mean, we're adults now."

Why *did* it bother me? I didn't have an answer for him. I could feel the heat rush to my face as a wave of embarrassment crashed over me. He's right, it did happen years ago. I should be over it by now.

Why can't I let it go?

I stood there, silent, for far longer than I should have. I didn't know what to do.

"Listen," Brandon said, pulling me out of my thoughts, "Why don't you let me make it up to you?"

"Make it up to me?" I eyed him suspiciously. He looked sincere, not like this was another of his pranks or anything. But still, you couldn't be too sure with him. "Why?"

He shrugged his shoulders. "Why not? I acted terrible towards you. So terrible that years later, you're still upset about it." My face grew even hotter. "Let me show you that I've changed. That I'm not the same person I was back then."

"How about this?" he said when I still hadn't responded, "Are you seeing anyone right now?"

"No, I'm not," I answered. I hated myself for answering him so quickly. I didn't want him knowing I was single. I didn't want him knowing anything about me.

Brandon smiled. "Good. I'm back in town because my sister is getting married. How would you like to accompany me? As my date?"

I'm sorry, his date? He can't be serious. Why

would I ever want to date him? Especially at a formal, family function like a wedding. That was just too much. The thought of us being seen together just at the bakery was embarrassing enough.

I looked up at him, ready to tell him no, to tell him off. But in this moment he looked so hopeful, so innocent. So. . . sexy. Not at all like the Brandon Cole that I had grown up with and come to hate.

I felt bad, almost guilty for turning him down.

But still . . .

"I don't think that's a good idea. But thank you," I added quickly. Before he could say anything else I was back in my car, heading towards home.

"Are you okay? Did something happen?" Mom asked as I set the pie down on the counter.

"George sent this home as a surprise. Said it looked like I needed it," I said, handing her the ice cream. I hoped it would be enough to distract her from any further questions. Brandon was the last thing I wanted to talk about right now.

"Oh, it's homemade," she exclaimed. "This is going to be great." She placed it in the freezer for later.

"But what happened?" She pressed. "Surely a tub of ice cream isn't what's gotten you all shaken up. You look like you've seen a ghost or something."

Close. "Brandon Cole," I answered. "I ran into him at the bakery."

Mom thought for a moment. "Brandon. I think I remember you having mentioned him once or twice over the years. How is he doing these days?"

Rich. Successful. Sexy as hell. "He seems to be doing alright. He's back for his sister's wedding."

"Oh, that's nice. I remember Clara. Such a sweet little thing." Unlike her brother.

"He invited me to the wedding."

"He did? Well, that's wonderful." My mom was beaming.

I nodded. It wasn't wonderful news though. Brandon was awful. Pretty much the devil if you asked me. "I told him I didn't think it was a good idea."

"Why on earth would you do a thing like that?" She practically yelled at me, causing me to wince. I didn't think it was such a big deal.

So I told her all about how he made my life a living hell, about how he basically was a monster towards me.

She looked at me, pity etched on her face. But instead of taking my side, she asked, "So you've been carrying that around with you all these years?"

I nodded slowly, suddenly feeling ashamed.

"What on earth could he have done that would cause you so much pain all this time? Surely, it wasn't that bad, or else you would have told me about it as soon as it happened."

"Well, he teased me, mocked everything I did, made me feel worthless . . . ," I began, feeling more ashamed by the second. It really did sound just like a teen being well, a teen boy.

"I think you should just give that man a chance," mom said, standing to finish dinner preparations. "It's been a long time, dear. Everyone changes."

Brandon

I HOPE I did the right thing. To be honest, I don't even know why I did it. It wasn't as if I had intended to invite Nina as my date to the wedding. Where my entire family would be gathered.

I was almost scared of what they might think, especially my mom. I never brought a girl home or to any family function, ever. Not even as a friend. She might read way too much into this. As she usually does.

Besides, I barely even remember Nina from high school. And the teasing? I mean, it does sound like me, like something I would have done. I'll be the first to admit that I was a little shit back then. Always getting into trouble, not caring who got hurt or what anyone thought.

That changed quickly after graduation though,

when I was expected to straighten up and take my place at one of our family's many companies. My family owned several highly successful real estate companies as well as law offices all over the country. The men in my family didn't play around. They didn't stick to just one profession or career. Hell, we even had a few bankers in the mix.

I never wanted any of that. I didn't want to be a part of that world. But it was expected of the men in this family to follow in their footsteps. No exception. Quitting any family business to forge your own path, follow your own dreams was practically forbidden. You'd be cast out as the black sheep, as an untrustworthy, disappointing embarrassment. Not only that but you'd be cut off from any and all family members, functions, anything. And money, forget any financial help. They'd rather see you broke and homeless than to not actively participate in the family business. You'd be permanently cut off from all family money. And from the family, period. Working in the family business was never something that I had wanted to do. But being cut off from everything and everyone was something I wanted even less. So I had to suck it up and work hard, pretending that I was okay with having most of my life already planned out for me.

Maybe that's why I acted out so much in school.

I'll be the first to admit that I acted like a little shit in school. I loved causing trouble, and didn't really seem to care who I hurt.

As long as I wasn't the one that was hurting.

Still, that was years ago. I'm not the same person I was back in high school, I've changed a lot since then. We all have. And I mean, I don't remember Nina ever looking like that. It's only been a few hours since we ran into each other, but I can't seem to get her off my mind. Not just because of her looks, either. The way she stood up to me, I thought it was a little sexy the way she did that.

Maybe she'll change her mind and come to the wedding.

Deep down, I really hoped she would. I couldn't imagine anyone else by my side. There was no one else I would want as my date.

Nina

❧

OVER THE NEXT few days I changed my mind more times than I could count about going to that damn wedding. It was all I could think about.

He was all I could think about.

And it drove me crazy.

Maybe if I just gave in and attended the wedding I could finally get him off my mind. I'll do him this favor and then never have to see his damn face ever again.

If only it was that easy.

I kicked myself for not asking for his phone number. Then again, the last time I saw Brandon I wanted nothing more than to get away from him.

All the back and forth was giving me a headache. I needed to lay down. I grabbed my phone to call Quinn as I rested. She was my best friend. She had been by my side all through school, she had seen first hand just how awful Brandon Cole really was. Maybe she could talk to my mom and get her to see my side of things.

She picked up on the first ring. "Hey, girly. How's life back at your moms?"

Well, straight to it, I see. She had always been like this though, so I shouldn't have been surprised. She always spoke her mind, whether you wanted to hear it or not.

"It's been . . . eventful," I admitted, letting out a small laugh.

"Eventful? Sounds interesting. So . . . spill." she said.

I filled her in on my little bakery adventure and also what my mother had said to me about it.

After a long silence I heard her suck in a breath. I waited to hear about how crappy Brandon is and more importantly, how right I was.

But that wasn't what was about to happen.

"Well babe," she began, "I hate to say this, but your mom is right."

"Um, what?" I asked, a little shocked.

"I mean, it's been years, Nina. It happened a long time ago. Usually people forget about most of what went on during their time in high school. I know I couldn't tell you anything that I did in school."

"Yeah, but . . ."

"No buts," she cut me off. "It's been long enough. It's way past time to let this go."

My heart sank. As much as I hated to admit it, I knew deep down that she was right. Her and my mom both. "I know," I finally admitted, my voice small. "I honestly don't know why the hell I held onto it for so long."

"I do."

"You do?"

"Of course. You have feelings for him," she said, like it should have been obvious this whole time.

I threw my head back and laughed. "You can't be serious. You can't actually believe that."

"I do. Think about it, why else would you still be affected by his actions? Why else would you be thinking about him all this time? There's no other explanation. You like him," he teased.

No, I don't. Quinn is wrong. So very wrong. She knows how he was and how much he tormented me and everything and . . .

Holy crap. I think I have feelings for him. How the hell did that happen? When did it happen?

"I take it from your silence that you agree with me?" Quinn asked.

"I, I don't know," I lied. I couldn't just tell her that

yeah, I agreed. I had spent so much time and energy hating the man. I wasn't quite ready to admit that the complete opposite might be true.

"Nina? Are you still there?"

"Yeah," I shoved the thoughts away. "Sorry, I was . . ."

"Thinking about your new possible boyfriend?" She teased.

"No," I lied again.

Quinn laughed. "Uh huh, sure. Well, I gotta go girly. Just promise me you'll think about what I said."

"Sure," I said softly before hanging up.

I tossed my phone near the end of my bed and sank down in the pillows. Could they be right? Was there a small chance that I actually did like him? The thought made me shiver. This couldn't be happening.

But still . . .

I needed to get out of here. I decided to go down to the park not that far from my house. Maybe a walk would help clear my head.

This park had always been a favorite place of mine to come, ever since I was a little girl. It started off as just a fun place to play, and turned into the place I went when I needed peace and quiet, somewhere to relax, or to just think. It had it all here - a section for dogs to run around and play, a large playground for children.

There were picnic tables and benches scattered along a pond that was sort of hidden along the edge of the park. And running around the outside of the park was a track that was popular with joggers and parents with young children that would push them in their strollers as they walked.

I usually spent most of my time sitting along the water's edge on my favorite bench. It was shaded by a large oak tree and was just so peaceful.

I was lost in thought, watching the ducks float around lazily on the surface of the water, and the occasional runner along the track. I hadn't seen Brandon approaching my bench and I jumped when he first spoke.

"Are you all right?" he asked, a smile tugging on his lips.

I put a hand on my chest, trying to steady my heart. "I am, yes," I answered. "What are you doing here?" As many times as I've come here over the years, I've never run into him even once.

"I was going for a run. It's a habit I've gotten into recently. It helps clear my head."

I nodded.

"What about you?" he asked, taking a seat beside me. It took everything I had not to scoot to the other side of the bench.

Clearing my throat, I answered him. "Same as you, basically. I like to come out here to think, clear my head." To be by myself.

"Speaking of," he turned his body towards me, "have you given it any more thought? The wedding, I mean."

A thousand thoughts swirled around in my head.

Have I thought about it? Only a million times a minute. It was all I could think about lately. But right now, looking at him, I couldn't think of a single reason not to go.

"Well?" he asked me gently.

I sucked in a deep breath. "Just one night?"

"Just one night," he nodded in agreement.

"Okay, fine. In that case, I'll go with you to the wedding."

A huge smile spread across his lips. "Great. I really think that we'll have a good time together. Also," he cleared his throat. "There is a huge family dinner the night before. I'd really like you to come to that as well."

So much for just one night.

I opened my mouth to protest, but he held up a hand to interrupt me. "I know, I know. I just got done telling you that it would only be one night. But you'd really be doing me a favor by doing this." He batted his eyelashes at me while pouting his mouth. He looked so ridiculous but I couldn't help laughing.

"Fine," I said. "But you owe me." Brandon leaned back on the bench, looking pleased with himself.

What the hell was I thinking?

Nina

"SO WHAT KIND of look are you going for?" Quinn asked as we looked through rack upon rack of fancy dresses.

"Not too sure," I said, putting back a hideous blue dress. "Nothing too sexy or revealing, that's for sure."

"Well, why not?" She pouted. "Don't you want to show him what he's been missing all these years?"

"You sound like he's an ex that I'm getting back at. And no. It's just a simple dinner."

"Yea, with his entire family," she rolled her eyes. "You should at least pretend to care. Try to impress them a little bit. Put a small amount of effort into your appearance at least."

Impress them? "Why though? It's just a fake date,"

I reminded her. "I doubt they would be impressed with that."

"They won't know it's a fake date," she pointed out. "To them it'll be real. Their son is bringing home a girl. That's usually a big deal."

A big deal? I didn't want his family thinking this was a big deal. That this thing between us was serious. I didn't want them to think this was anything more than just a simple date. Because honestly, that's all it was Nothing more. And I had to somehow make sure they knew that.

After about an hour more of shopping I decided on a simple pale yellow dress that hugged my curves in a modest kind of way. Sexy yet acceptable for meeting the parents.

When Brandon picked me up I was a ball of nerves. Meeting a boyfriend's parents for the first time was nerve wracking on a normal day. This was beyond that. Not only was I meeting his parents but I had to pretend to be his happy-in-love girlfriend. I just hoped I'd be able to pull it off.

"How are you feeling?" Brandon asked, as if sensing my nervousness.

"I'm fine," I lied. "I'm just wondering what your family is going to think of me."

"There's nothing to worry about," he said with a reassuring tone, "they are going to love you."

"But how are we going to convince them that we are so happy and in love?"

"You just leave that to me," Brandon laughed. "We'll be fine. Promise."

I sure hoped so. I guess I had no other choice but to trust him.

We got to his parents house, and I don't know why, but for some reason the sight of all the cars in the driveway made me really nervous. I really wished we could just turn around and drive away. I would be happy going anywhere, anywhere but here.

Brandon walked around the car to open the door for me and I briefly considered locking myself inside. I had the worst luck with meeting the parents on a good day, with someone that I was actually in love with. How on Earth was I supposed to convince these people that I was madly in love with Brandon? I was never really good at lying.

But dinner went better than I could have imagined. His family was warm and welcoming. They were all shocked when Brandon walked into the house with a girl. It made me wonder if I was the first.

If I was, that really would be a huge deal.

I mostly tried to sit back and listen as his family

members took turns telling embarrassing stories about Brandon, or telling me how Clara and Steven met. They talked about the wedding and how excited they were.

Brandon also showed me a different side of him that I didn't know existed. The Brandon I knew from way back when was cold, rude, obnoxious. The man I sat next to tonight was just like his family - warm, friendly, he even seemed loving and caring towards his family.

Who the hell was he?

As I watched him interact with the young kids running around I felt myself falling for him.

This could be a problem. But could Quinn be right after all? I wasn't ready for that possibility.

I just needed to get through the night.

THE WEDDING WAS ABSOLUTELY BEAUTIFUL. I don't think I've ever witnessed so much love in one room before. I never heard a word anyone said during the ceremony though. My attention was focused purely on Brandon. He looked so sexy standing up there as a groomsman. His dark blue suit fit him perfectly. I found my thoughts wandering, wondering how it would feel to undo those buttons on his shirt, running my hands along his abs. Snaking my hands through his hair as I …

I shook the thoughts away, face burning from embarrassment. Sneaking a quick glance up at Brandon, I noticed he was watching me with a smile on his face. I just hope that nothing on my own face had given away what had been on my mind. I didn't need him to know what I was thinking. I didn't even know how he felt about me.

Well, that was a lie. Brandon felt nothing for me. I was just here for . . . why the hell was I here? I can't recall any mention of him wanting to get his family off his back or even just to show them that he is capable of a relationship. Nothing like that. So why?

My heart did a backflip and I watched Brandon, raking my eyes over every inch of his perfect body. Could he actually like me? Even a little bit? Is that why he brought me here? To a huge family event? Could this really be the start of something amazing?

Where the hell was Quinn when I needed her? She was the one that pointed out the fact that I had hidden feelings for him. One look and she'd be able to tell how he felt about me.

If he even felt anything about me at all.

The ceremony ended and as Clara and Steven walked down the aisle as husband and wife, I couldn't help but notice how flawless she looked. She had a dreamy look in her eyes that had her practically floating. It was painfully obvious how in love those two were. I hope to someday have half of the happiness that they did.

All the bridesmaids and groomsmen made their way after them. Brandon only had eyes for me as he made his way past, throwing me a quick wink and that sexy smile of his as he walked by.

Maybe my own happiness wasn't that far away after all.

Once they announced it was time for pictures I stood off to the side, out of the way. Apparently I wasn't as out of the way as I hoped because I heard Brandon's mother calling me.

"Come on, Nina. Join us," she called, waving her arms wildly. I just shook my head and stared down at my feet. I really didn't want to be in their family photos. They would all be ruined when the truth came out that Brandon and I were lying about us being together.

As his mother kept calling for me I felt strong arms around me. "Come on," Brandon whispered. "Just a couple pictures. It'll be okay," he assured me.

"Fine," I gave in, trying to keep a smile on my face. I didn't want to cause any drama on Clara's special day. I don't know how long I was going to be able to keep this up. How would I be able to hide my real feelings for Brandon when they're going to forever be captured in these photos?

I took a deep breath and put on my best fake smile. I had to keep reminding myself that this was all just pretend.

No matter how much I wish it was real.

Brandon

CLEARLY, I hadn't thought this through. In my mind, Nina and I would go to the wedding, have a great time, and get everyone off my back about always being single. I thought that we would be able to convince my family that we were together and happy and that would be that.

But man, was I wrong.

Instead of fooling everyone else, we seemed to be only fooling ourselves.

I had had a crush on Nina since way back in school. It was part of the reason I treated her the way I did back then. I was part of the so-called 'cool' people, and she wasn't. So if any of my friends were to find out that I liked her, that would be it for me. I'd be dead.

So I had to play it cool, pretend I felt nothing but

disgust for her. Maybe I ended up taking things too far. That's why she carried that anger and hurt around with her all these years.

I had to make things right.

As I was one of the groomsmen I couldn't sit with Nina during the ceremony. I felt bad leaving her on her own. Besides my family, that she had just met, I don't think she knew a single other person here.

I watched her from my place up near the front of the church, hoping it wasn't too obvious. I had to admit, she looked sexy in that rose pink colored dress she chose. I only knew what color it was because she told me, like it was something I cared about.

When it came time for pictures, I noticed Nina trying to hide away off to the side. It was kind of funny. The family was all lined up, the photographer snapped a couple and then my mother stopped him.

"Nina!" She called out to my date. I looked over at her to see her face turn a few shades darker than her dress. I looked down and tried to hide my smile. "Come join us."

I leaned over toward my mother. "What are you doing?" I whispered.

"She should be in at least one picture," she said, looking at me with a huge smile on her face. "The way you two have been looking at each other all day, I just have a really good feeling about it," she said, looking like she was starting to tear up. "You look so happy together," she beamed.

I felt my gut twist with guilt. I really hated lying to my mother. She was so excited over the idea of me and Nina.

If I'm being honest, so was I.

But I knew how she felt about me. And it was definitely the opposite of what I was feeling for her.

Not wanting to disappoint her more than I already had, I stepped out of my spot in the lineup and convinced Nina to take at least one picture with us.

What was the worst that could happen?

As she stood close to my side I slid my arm around her. I felt her body tense for a second then relax.

It only took a minute or so for her to warm back up, continuing to go along with our plan. My plan. I don't remember whose it was at this point. All I knew was that I loved having her next to me.

And I never wanted to let her go.

The reception was no better. The open bar and the romantic atmosphere did not help at all. It was a dangerous mix.

I was chatting with Charlie, another one of the groomsmen, when I noticed Nina out of the corner of my eye. She seemed to be stuck with one of my relatives. I didn't get a good look at who it was until he turned his face slightly.

Shit.

"I'll catch up with you in a bit," I told Charlie, and headed off towards Nina. The poor girl had gotten herself cornered by Uncle Roger. I loved Uncle Roger, sure. But he was somewhat of a pig. He loved younger, sexy women and once he had his sights on someone he would not quit until he got what he wanted.

It looked like I caught him just in time. "Hey there Uncle Roger. How did you like the ceremony?"

He looked at me in surprise. "Brandon. There you are. I haven't seen you in, what? Years now?"

Three wonderful years.

I nodded. "That's right. Now," I moved closer, sliding my arm around Nina's waist. "I hope you don't mind but I'd like to steal my girlfriend for a dance."

She smiled up at me, relief spread across her face. I nodded once to Roger and then led Nina out to the dance floor.

"I thought the whole creepy-Uncle-at-the-reception thing wasn't real," she laughed. "I thought it was just made up."

"I wish it was," I said. I twirled her once and then pulled her close to me as a slow song began to play. For a second she looked like she was about to turn around and walk away from me. I panicked a little, not wanting her to leave. I never wanted her to leave. But she quickly relaxed, and melted into my arms.

She even looked like she might be enjoying herself.

Dancing with her like this, holding her in my arms, it felt right. As the night wore on, we shared a few drinks as well as a few more dances. I could feel myself falling more and more in love with her.

Nina

SUNLIGHT FILTERED through the half open curtains, waking me up. I stretched., and my hand hit something. I looked over to see Brandon, still asleep, lying next to me.

Then it all came rushing back.

The dancing, the alcohol, the creepy uncle. Brandon telling me he liked me.

I sat bolt upright. Holy shit. Brandon Cole said he liked me. I felt giddy at that thought. This all started out as pretend, but maybe it was turning into something real. Could Brandon really have feelings for me? Or was it the alcohol talking?

I tried not to get my hopes up just in case, but after spending time with him, I found myself really falling for him. If he loved me back . . .

Plus, here I was in his bed. After spending the night together. One hot, steamy night. He wouldn't just do that with anyone, right? He wouldn't have sex with me and then throw me away the next day,

Right?

Brandon began to stir. "Morning," he said through a yawn.

"Morning."

He got up to change so he could take me home, and I hunted for my clothes that had been thrown all over the room.

Just how wild did last night get?

"So," Brandon said, once we had started off towards my house, "did you have a good time yesterday?"

"The best," I admitted. I had much more fun than I ever thought I could with Brandon.

He just nodded, keeping his eyes on the road. I wish that I could tell what he was thinking.

I cleared my throat, deciding just to go for it and ask him. "So what do you think about us getting together again? For coffee or dinner or whatever?"

He shifted slightly in his seat. "I don't think it's a good idea."

My heart stopped. "What? Why?" I asked, voice shaking.

"Well, this was just supposed to be one night, remember? Your words."

Yes, I remember. But that changed. Once I actually spent time with you and got to know you a little bit.

"Well yes, but . . ."

"I think we should stick to our original agreement," he said, in a tone that said he was done talking about this.

So the rest of the ride home was spent in silence. When we arrived at my house I didn't even bother saying goodbye, just hopped out, tears streaming down my face.

Brandon

I fucked up. I fucked up bad. Why the hell did I tell her no to dating when it was all I thought about at the wedding? There was something seriously wrong with me. I mean, a beautiful girl, who I have feelings for, spends the night with me and then asks to see me again. And I turned her down.

Why?

Part of me was hesitant because, after all, it was her idea for this to be just one night. She had told me she didn't want more. She had no idea how I really felt, but would that really matter?

I remembered the first day we ran into each other again, the anger that was burning in her eyes. There was something oddly sexy about that, a woman who is passionate I suppose. I invited her to the wedding because I wanted to be around her more.

I wanted her to be mine.

So why did I have to go and mess this all up? All I could think about was the tears streaming down her face as I dropped her off.

I felt bad.

I felt like an ass.

I'm supposed to be heading out of town for a while for work, but maybe I could just put it all off for a bit, until I figure things out with Nina. Because there's no way I can leave things like this.

After days of her ignoring my phone I decide the best thing to do is drive to her house and try to get her to talk to me face to face

I knocked and her mother ended up answering the door. "Brandon. What brings you by?" she asked cheerfully. It was nice to know that at least she didn't hate me.

"I was actually hoping to speak to your daughter, if she's here. She hasn't been picking up her phone and I have something important I would like to discuss with her."

She opened the door wider. "Well, come on in. She's hiding back in her room. I'll take you to her."

"Thank you," I said, following her.

"So what happened at the wedding?" she asked.

I shook my head. "That's what I'm hoping to find out," I answered.

She led me to a door. "Here it is. Nina's room. Go on ahead," she gestured to the door and left me standing there. I knocked as I slowly opened it.

Nina was sitting at a small wooden desk, just kind of staring off into space. "Brandon!" she exclaimed when she finally noticed me. She had her hand over her chest, like I startled her.

"What are you doing here?" she asked.

"I wanted to talk to you. You weren't answering your phone."

"I didn't think I needed to."

Fair. She was hurt.

I decided before coming here that I wasn't going to beat around the bush anymore. That I would just come right out and spell things out for her.

"I'm sorry for the way I treated you," I began. "Honestly, I have no idea why I acted like that. Actually, no. I do know." I said, finding my confidence.

"Care to tell me?" She said, a little bite in her voice.

Okay, I deserved that.

I moved closer to her. "I did it because I was scared. It was stupid of me, I know. But, I've never felt this way about anyone before, Nina."

"Like what?"

"I'm falling in love with you."

She stared at me, like she didn't know what to say. So I just continued.

I took a seat on the edge of her bed. "If I'm being completely honest, I have had a crush on you for a while now. For years."

"You have?" She asked, clearly confused.

"Since high school."

"Since high school?!" She asked, voice growing louder. "Then why did you treat me the way you did? How can you say that you liked me when you made my life a living hell?"

"It was because I liked you that I did that. I know, it doesn't make any sense. But I was young and . . ."

"A dumbass," she finished for me.

"Yea," I agreed. "A dumbass. And I was one again the day after the wedding. I was scared back then, and I had no idea how you felt about me. From day one you made it perfectly clear that you wanted nothing to do with me after the wedding."

She looked down at her feet, looking shy. It was adorable. I wanted to wrap my arms around her. "I said that because I was sure that's what you wanted. At first, it was what I wanted. But then I met your family, and got to know you. And after a while I realized that I had feelings for you, too."

I breathed out a long, slow breath. "So what do you say? Can we start over? Let me make this up to you. Again. But with a proper date this time, just the two of us?"

She got up out of her chair and walked over to me, stopping in front of me. "I would love to go on a date with you," she said. "But not starting over. I want to go as your girlfriend."

My heart jumped. "Seriously?"

Seriously." she nodded and jumped in my lap, kissing me like there was no tomorrow.